This book belongs to:

Stewart

AUTUMN
PUBLISHING

Published in 2020
by Autumn Publishing
Cottage Farm
Sywell
NN6 0BJ
www.igloobooks.com

Autumn is an imprint of Bonnier Books UK

0120 001
2 4 6 8 10 9 7 5 3 1
ISBN 978-1-83903-054-3

Printed and manufactured in China

Long ago, the world was full of wonder, adventure and best of all… magic!

Wizards used magic for absolutely everything – from lighting dark rooms and mystical caves with bright, glowing orbs to battling ferocious, fire-breathing dragons while on noble quests.

But magic was very hard to learn and took lots of practice. Eventually, technology took over from the old ways. It was much easier to light a room by flicking a switch than performing a spell.

Because of this, magic was now a thing of the past.

Ian Lightfoot was a shy teenage elf who lived with his mum and brother in a town called New Mushroomton. Ian was more concerned about making friends and fitting in at school than he was about magic and heading off on glorious adventures.

Today was Ian's sixteenth birthday. As he came downstairs that morning, he was jumped on and licked by his excited pet dragon, Blazey. She was always happy to see him.

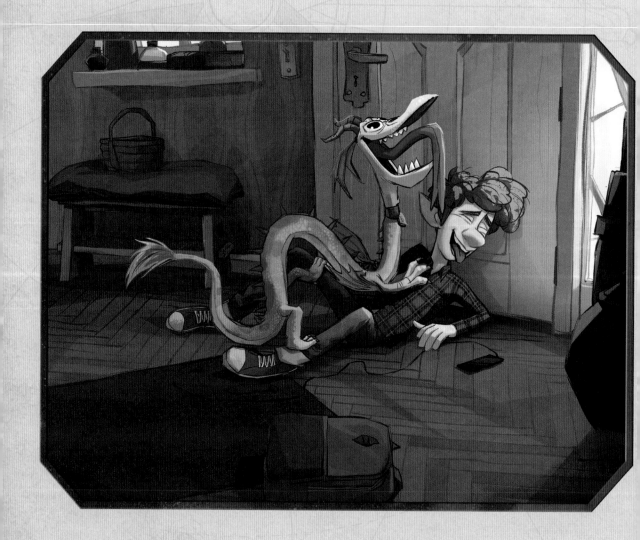

Ian made his way to the kitchen. As he was about to move a board game off
the table, his older brother, Barley, suddenly pulled him into a headlock.
"Doth my brother dare disrupt an active campaign?" demanded Barley.
He spent countless hours playing Quests of Yore, a game based on real magic.
Barley was obsessed with the past, but Ian found it strange and embarrassing.

After a long day at school, Ian was in his room.

He was feeling down and wished he could have been more like his dad, who had passed away when Ian was very young.

Ian thought about all the things he wanted to do but couldn't, as he wasn't bold or confident like his dad had been.

Ian clicked on an old tape recording of his dad's voice. He played it so often he had it memorised. Ian liked to speak in between his dad's sentences as though they were having a conversation. More than anything, Ian wished he could talk to his dad for real.

That evening, Laurel – Ian and Barley's mum – sat with Ian as he mended his sweatshirt that had been accidentally ripped earlier in the day. She could tell he had been thinking about his father and was feeling down. So, to cheer him up, she revealed an exciting surprise: Ian and Barley's dad had left a special gift for them. It was only to be opened when both of the boys had turned sixteen.

Ian and Barley were shocked when they unwrapped a real wizard's staff! It came with a rare Phoenix Gem and a Visitation Spell that would bring their father back for one day.

Barley placed the gem in the staff and recited the spell. "Only once is all we get, grant me this rebirth. 'Til tomorrow's sun has set, one day to walk the earth!"

Nothing happened. Barley tried over and over again, but it was no use.

Everyone was disappointed, but none more so than Ian. Alone in his room, he read the spell out loud. Suddenly, the Phoenix Gem glowed. Ian grabbed the staff and a beam of light shot out!

Barley arrived just as their father's shoes and socks began to materialise. Ian struggled to hold the staff steady. Barley tried to help, but the gem exploded, throwing the boys to the floor! They thought the spell had failed until they heard something rustling in the wardrobe…

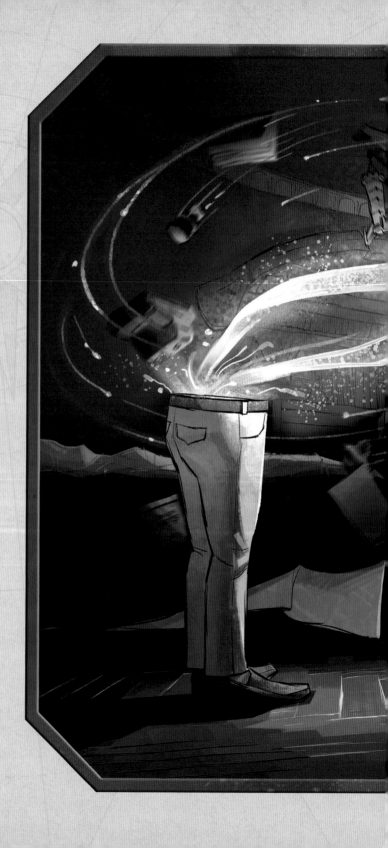

It was their dad – but only his bottom half! His legs stood up and
staggered around. Ian was upset to see his father's confusion, but Barley
tapped out a rhythm on Dad's shoe, just like he'd done as a child.
Dad tapped his foot in reply! Then Dad placed his foot on Ian's.
He knew his sons were there with him.

Barley was thrilled that his little brother had the magic gift. Now they needed to find another Phoenix Gem so they could retry the spell before sunset. But first they had to get a map so they would know where to look for a new Phoenix Gem.

"We'll start at the place where all quests begin," said Barley. "The Manticore's Tavern!"

Ian had his doubts, but he was willing to try anything. The three Lightfoot men all piled into Guinevere – Barley's van – and drove off. Along the way, Ian used old clothes to make an upper body for their dad.

Laurel returned home and found a note on Ian's door promising her a big surprise. Seeing his messy room, Laurel knew something had happened. Finding out her sons were heading to the Manticore's Tavern, she grabbed her keys and ran back to her car.

In the meantime, Barley handed Ian the Quests of Yore players' guide so he could practise magic. Ian started off by trying the Levitation Spell but couldn't make it work.

Barley told him to speak from his Heart's Fire. "You've gotta speak with passion. Don't hold back!"

"Aloft Elevar!" exclaimed Ian once more, taking his brother's advice. But it still didn't work.

  As they approached the tavern, Barley insisted that he'd do all the talking. The Manticore, a legendary thousand-year-old warrior, had to be treated with the proper respect.

Barley, Ian and Dad were surprised to discover that the tavern – once filled with thrill-seeking adventurers undertaking quests of great peril – was now a family-friendly restaurant featuring birthday parties and karaoke. And the Manticore, now better known as Corey, was no longer the fearsome beast spoken about in legend.

Barley knelt before Corey and asked for the map. She refused to give them the real one. Instead, Corey offered them a children's menu that was based on the map. The Manticore now believed quests were dangerous and, if someone got hurt, she could lose her tavern.

Barley reminded the Manticore that she used to take risks and lived for adventure. Realising she was living a lie, the Manticore cried out, "WHAT HAVE I BECOME?" She then blew fire all around the tavern, burning everything that was modern about the restaurant.

The customers ran for the exits. Ian tried to grab the map, but it was lost in the fire.

Suddenly, a flaming wooden beam cracked in two and fell towards Dad! Ian raised the wizard's staff and cried, "Aloft Elevar!"

This time, the Levitation Spell worked! The beam hovered right above his father. Barley pulled Dad to safety and the trio ran back to the van.

Using the menu the Manticore gave them, Barley found a clue that led to Raven's Point. Barley wanted to take the ancient Path of Peril, like in one of his games, but Ian wanted to spend as much time with Dad as possible and insisted they take the expressway, which would be quicker. Barley reluctantly agreed.

Meanwhile, Laurel arrived at the burning tavern where the Manticore told her about the boys' quest to find a Phoenix Gem. The tavern owner then remembered about the Phoenix Gem Curse – which she'd forgotten to mention to Barley and Ian. Laurel quickly drove them both away from the tavern. The Manticore explained they had to get the only thing that would help against the curse – her enchanted sword, the Curse Crusher!

Back at the van, Ian, Barley and Dad were in trouble. Guinevere had run out of petrol and spluttered to a stop. To make matters worse, Barley's petrol can was almost empty and there was no petrol station in sight.

Barley suggested the Growth Spell might help. The can would grow bigger and so would the petrol inside!

Casting the spell required intense focus. Ian held up the staff and recited, "Magnora Gantuan!" The can started to grow! But after Ian became distracted by Barley and the magic, the spell backfired. Now Barley was tiny!

After finding a petrol station, Ian began filling up the petrol can. Just as he finished, he heard Dewdrop – the leader of a motorcycle club of tough-talking sprites called the Pixie Dusters – arguing with Barley. Ian apologised to the sprites and pulled his tiny brother away. Then, Dad accidentally bumped into the Pixie Dusters' motorcycles. One by one, the bikes fell over!

The sprites were furious! Ian, Barley and Dad ran away from Dewdrop and his motorcycle club as fast as they could.

Back in Guinevere, the boys faced a new problem: Barley was too small to drive! Ian had no choice but to get behind the wheel himself if they were to escape the sprites and reach the expressway. However, Ian was terrified about joining the moving traffic.

With his brother's help, Ian overcame his fear and drove Guinevere onto the expressway. But the Pixie Dusters caught up with them! They were getting closer when Ian swerved across several lanes of traffic towards their exit. They had soon left the expressway and escaped the sprites!

They hadn't gone far before the police pulled them over. Ian and Barley, who had returned to normal size, quickly came up with a plan.

Ian used the Disguise Spell to cloak himself and Barley in an image of Officer Bronco – their mum's boyfriend. But the spell came with a rule: if Ian lied, a part of the disguise would disappear.

The plan was working until one of the officers called Barley a screw-up. When Ian disagreed, one leg of the disguise vanished. Barley knew Ian had lied.

Having got away from the police, the three of them drove in silence until they reached a place where they could stop and rest. Ian tried to explain that he didn't think his brother was a screw-up. Barley wouldn't listen. Instead, he turned the music on, turned up the volume and got out of the van. He knew magic didn't lie.

"I don't know how any of this stuff works!" exclaimed Ian. "All I know is that everything we've done tonight has gone wrong!"

"It's gone wrong because you won't listen to me!" replied Barley.

Suddenly, Dad started dancing to the vibrations of the music blasting from Guinevere! He strutted over to the boys and got them dancing, too.

With the tension broken, Barley said he wanted a chance to prove himself. Ian agreed to do things his way. They would travel to the Path of Peril!

At the same time, the Manticore and Laurel arrived at the pawn shop where the Manticore had sold her enchanted sword years before.

"Hello, old friend," the Manticore said to the Curse Crusher. "Forged of the rarest metals, the only sword of its kind in all the land."

Hearing about the sword's value, the greedy owner, Grecklin, increased the price! Desperate, the Manticore stung Grecklin with her scorpion tail! The Manticore promised the effects would soon wear off. Laurel dropped some money on the counter, and the duo ran out with the sword.

Meanwhile, Ian, Barley and Dad had arrived at a drawbridge. With Barley's support, Ian used a Trust Bridge Spell to reach the other side. Once there, Ian lowered the bridge so Barley could drive across. When they were all safely on the other side, they saw a statue of a raven. Barley realised that the clue wasn't leading them to Raven's Point; it was telling them to go where the ravens were pointing. Sure enough, when they looked in the direction the statue pointed, they could see another raven in the distance.

Ian was impressed. Maybe his brother had been right all along.

As Ian sped through the winding mountain roads, police cars suddenly appeared and began to chase them. Ian turned a corner sharply to try and escape them, but they came to a dead end. Barley told Ian to block the road by hitting an outcropping of boulders with Arcane Lightning, the most difficult spell in the Quests of Yore players' guide.

"Voltar Thundasir!" shouted Ian. Nothing happened.

With the police closing in, Barley made a difficult decision. After getting everyone out of the van, he put a rock on Guinevere's accelerator pedal and directed the van at the boulders. Guinevere raced ahead and flew through the air before crashing into the rocks, creating a landslide that blocked the road. They'd escaped the police, but Barley's precious van was now buried under the rubble.

The three of them continued their journey on foot. Following where the ravens were pointing, they eventually came to a raven that stood near a river. There was a loose stone on the raven, which Barley pulled out. The strange symbol on the stone gave him an idea.

"We go to the end of the water, and we'll find that Phoenix Gem," said Barley.

Ian, Barley and Dad followed the river into a cave. Using magic, Ian made a raft from one of Barley's cheese puffs. Then, they sped down the river. Along the way, Ian practised other spells. He felt more confident that he would be able to perform the Visitation Spell again and finally meet his dad.

At that moment, Barley shared a sad memory with Ian. When their dad was in hospital, Barley was too scared to go into his room to say goodbye.

Barley sighed. "That's when I decided I was never gonna be scared again."

The river ended at the entrance to the Final Gauntlet. Barley said the Phoenix Gem would be on the other side. But getting to it wouldn't be easy.

The brothers grabbed shields from the floor and, holding Dad between them, ran through the tunnel. Arrows, swords and flames came at them from every direction!

They entered a small chamber and slammed the door shut. Suddenly, water began to fill the room! The boys guided Dad underwater to a star-shaped tile that opened a portal in the ceiling. The portal opened and they escaped just in time!

"The Phoenix Gem awaits beyond this door!" exclaimed Barley.

Ian laughed. "Dad, we have followed the quest and it has led us to our victory!"

The group climbed through the portal into the sunlight above.

But they soon discovered they were back in New Mushroomton, right where they'd started.

"No, that doesn't make sense!" exclaimed Barley. "This has to be where the Phoenix Gem is. I followed my gut."

Ian was crushed. He'd trusted his brother and it had got them nowhere. Now he'd never get to meet his dad. "You act like you know what you're doing, but you don't have a clue," Ian said to Barley. "That's because… you are a screw-up!"

Ian turned and walked into the park with Dad, leaving Barley alone.

Ian sat on a cliff as the sun began to set and pulled out the list of things he'd wanted to do with his father. He was about to scribble them all out when Ian realised something. He'd already done them all – not with Dad, but with Barley!

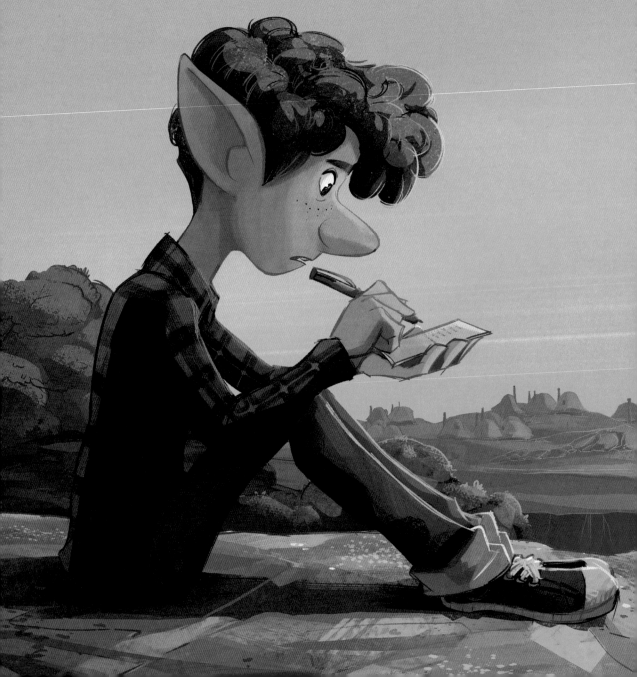

He thought about all the times during his life that his brother had encouraged him, had fun with him and helped him become a better person. Barley had always been there for Ian. Now Ian would return the favour.

In the meantime, Barley noticed that the stone from the raven statue fit perfectly in the old fountain. After he placed the stone into the fountain, it opened up and a hidden chamber revealed the Phoenix Gem!

Ian returned to help, but suddenly, a smoky mist poured out of the fountain. It was the curse!

The mist tore apart the high school and used the pieces to form a massive dragon. The fire-breathing beast stomped towards Barley!

"Run!" he shouted to Ian and Dad.

Just then, a dark shape swooped down from the sky. It was the Manticore wielding the Curse Crusher – with Laurel riding on her back! While looking for her children, Laurel had discovered she could be a mighty warrior just like the Manticore.

While Laurel and the Manticore battled the dragon, Ian put the Phoenix Gem in place and cast the Visitation Spell. This caught the dragon's attention. Barley wanted to distract it so Ian could finally meet Dad.

"No!" exclaimed Ian. "You say goodbye. I had someone who looked out for me, someone who pushed me to be more than I ever thought I could be. I never had a dad... but I always had you."

Ian grabbed the staff and sprinted towards the dragon. He hit it with Arcane Lightning, knocking away its outer armour. Laurel tossed the Curse Crusher to him and Ian used another spell to plunge the enchanted sword deep into the curse. The dragon exploded in a blinding flash, causing debris to fly everywhere.

Ian was trapped beneath the rubble. Suddenly, there was another burst of light. Peeking through the debris, Ian could see Dad fully materialising in front of Barley. Tears filled Ian's eyes as Barley and Dad talked and laughed. As the sun dropped below the horizon, Dad hugged Barley and then disappeared in his arms.

Barley made his way to Ian and helped him out of the rubble. He told his brother how proud Dad was of the person Ian had become.

Ian smiled. "Well, I owe an awful lot of that to you."

"He kinda said that, too," said Barley. "Oh, and he told me to give you this." Barley gave his brother a big hug.

After their adventure with Dad, life for Ian and Barley changed.

Ian used magic to rebuild the school and made lots of new friends. He also used magic to give Barley's new van, Guinevere the Second, a custom paint job!

Barley wanted to take her for a spin to the park through the Road of Ruin.

"Too obvious," said Ian. "On a quest, the clear path is never the right one." Then Guinevere the Second lifted off the ground and began to fly!

"Yeah!" shouted Barley.

The quest had changed the Lightfoot family. Each of them had discovered
things about themselves they hadn't known before. And the experience of seeing
Dad return, even briefly, had brought the family closer together than ever.
No matter what was to come, they would always have each other to lean on.